ni hao, kai-lan

NICKELODEON

D0594983

Wait, Hoho, Wait!

adapted by Alison Inches

based on the screenplay written by Joe Purdy

illustrated by Daniel Mather

Ready-to-Read

SIMON SPOTLIGHT/NICKELODEON

New York   London   Toronto   Sydney

Based on the TV series *Ni Hao, Kai-lan*™ as seen on Nickelodeon®

SIMON SPOTLIGHT
An imprint of Simon & Schuster Children's Publishing Division
1230 Avenue of the Americas, New York, New York 10020

Copyright © 2009 Viacom International Inc. All rights reserved. NICKELODEON, *Ni Hao, Kai-lan!*, and all related titles,
logos, and characters are trademarks of Viacom International Inc.
All rights reserved, including the right of reproduction in whole or in part in any form.
SIMON SPOTLIGHT, READY-TO-READ, and colophon are registered trademarks of Simon & Schuster, Inc.

Manufactured in the United States of America
10 9
Library of Congress Cataloging-in-Publication Data
Inches, Alison.
Wait, Hoho, wait! / adapted by Alison Inches ; from a teleplay by Joe
Purdy. — 1st ed.
p. cm. — (Ready-to-read)
"Based on the TV series Ni Hao Kai-lan as seen on Nick Jr."— Copyright
page.
ISBN 978-1-4169-8519-8
0610 LAK
I. Purdy, Joe. II. Ni Hao Kai-lan (Television program) III. Title.
PZ7.I355Wai 2009
[E — dc22
2008050143

Ni hao! I'm .
KAI-LAN

Today 🐯 got a new toy 🚗!
RINTOO · CAR

🐵 wants to ride in the 🚗 right now.
HOHO · CAR

Not yet, .
HOHO

 and  have to
RINTOO   TOLEE

build the  first.
CAR

The  has lots of parts.
CAR

It will take some time.

HOHO watches RINTOO and TOLEE.

They put the CAR parts

on the ground.

They have , a  ,  ,
DOORS   STEERING WHEEL   HEADLIGHTS

, and a  .
WHEELS   MIRROR

"Is the  ready yet?" asks  .
CAR   HOHO

"Not yet!" say  and  .
RINTOO   TOLEE

 really wants to ride
HOHO

in the toy .
CAR

He stomps his feet and hops up

and down.

Then he jumps in the toy .
CAR

Crash!

The
CAR
falls apart.

Oh, no!

HOHO did not know how to wait.

and will have to start over.
RINTOO   TOLEE

is very sorry.
HOHO

How can  learn how to wait?
HOHO

Hey, look at .
YEYE

When he has to wait, he does

something he likes. He sings.

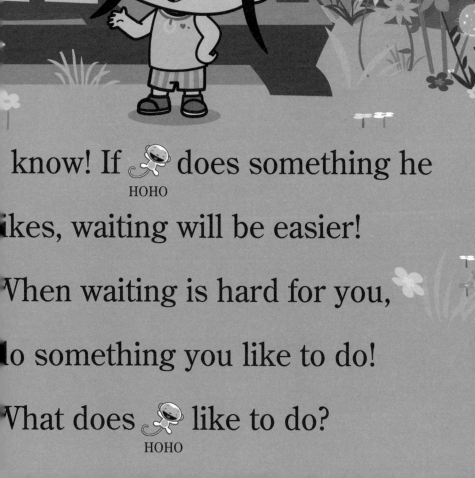

know! If does something he
HOHO

ikes, waiting will be easier!

When waiting is hard for you,

o something you like to do!

Vhat does like to do?
HOHO

likes to play "Where's HOHO ?"
HOHO

Is HOHO in the SHED ?

No!

Is  in the 🎃 patch?

HOHO   PUMPKIN

No!

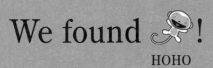

Is 🐵 in the 🌳?
HOHO   TREE
Yes!

We found 🐵!
HOHO

"Is the  ready yet?" asks .

CAR   HOHO

"Not yet," say  and .

RINTOO   TOLEE

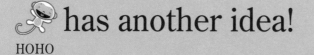 has another idea!

HOHO

He will build a rock tower.

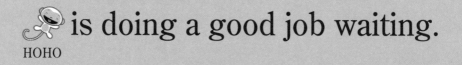 is doing a good job waiting.

HOHO

"Is the  ready yet?" asks .
CAR   HOHO

"Not yet!" say and .
RINTOO   TOLEE

 has another idea.

HOHO

He plays music on his  .

TURNTABLES

"Is the  ready?" asks .
CAR   HOHO

"Yes! The  is done!"
CAR

say  and .
RINTOO   TOLEE

Wow!  did a super job waiting.

HOHO

Now all we need is a push.

Can you help us?

Say "Push!"

Here we go!

What a super !
CAR

Thanks for helping  learn
HOHO

how to wait.

You make my  feel super happy!
HEART